# A SPOTLIGHT FOR HARRY

by ERIC A. KIMMEL

illustrated by JIM MADSEN

A STEPPING STONE BOOK™

Random House 🏠 New York

*For Gavin and Grady—E.A.K.*
*For Easton, the best magician I know—J.M.*

Text copyright © 2009 by Eric Kimmel
Illustrations copyright © 2009 by James Madsen

Published in the United States by Random House Children's Books, a division
of Random House, Inc., New York. Originally published in hardcover in the
United States by Random House Children's Books in 2009.

Random House and the colophon are registered trademarks and A Stepping
Stone Book and the colophon are trademarks of Random House, Inc.

Visit us on the Web!
SteppingStonesBooks.com
www.randomhouse.com/kids

Educators and librarians, for a variety of teaching tools, visit us at
www.randomhouse.com/teachers

*Library of Congress Cataloging-in-Publication Data*
Kimmel, Eric A.
A spotlight for Harry / by Eric A. Kimmel ; illustrated by Jim Madsen.
p.   cm.
"A Stepping Stone book."
ISBN 978-0-375-85869-7 (trade) — ISBN 978-0-375-95869-4 (lib. bdg.) —
ISBN 978-0-375-85696-9 (pbk.)
1. Houdini, Harry, 1874–1926—Juvenile literature. 2. Magicians—United
States—Biography—Juvenile literature. 3. Escape artists—United States—
Biography—Juvenile literature. I. Madsen, Jim, ill. II. Title.
GV1545.H8K56 2009   793.8092—dc22   [B]   2008052473

Printed in the United States of America
10 9 8 7 6 5 4 3 2 1

# CONTENTS

# THE CIRCUS

"**H**urry, Dash!" Harry Weiss called to his younger brother. "Can't you all go any faster? We're never going to get good seats if we don't hurry. We may even miss the whole show!"

"Slow down, Ehrich! You too, Dezso," Rabbi Weiss told the boys. "The show doesn't start for an hour. Besides, how do you expect Mama to run when she has to walk with Leopold and carry Gladys? We'll get there in plenty of time, and we'll have wonderful seats."

Harry and Dash stopped to wait for their family. "Trust me," their father went on. "Nobody knows better than Mayer Samuel Weiss how to get good seats at the circus. Who knows? If life had turned out differently, I might have been a circus performer myself. Can you see me as a lion tamer? Or a trapeze artist flying through the air high above the center ring? I've never missed a circus in my life, even when I was a boy in Hungary."

"And now that you're a grown man and a rabbi in America, you still act like a boy when the circus comes to town," said Mrs. Weiss. She carried Harry and Dash's little sister in her arms. Their younger brother, Leopold, toddled along beside her, holding tightly on to her hand.

Rabbi Weiss and his family were important

members of the small, but growing, Jewish community in Appleton, Wisconsin. Like many new immigrants, Rabbi and Mrs. Weiss spoke little English. Rabbi Weiss's Saturday-morning sermons at the synagogue were in German. German was the main language the Weiss family spoke at home. They all spoke German now, on their way to the circus.

The two older boys, Harry and Dash, spoke German with their parents. However, between themselves, they spoke English. Although they had been born in Hungary, they thought of themselves as Americans. They gave themselves American names.

Ehrich's nickname at home was Ehri. At school, it became Harry. Dezso easily became Dash.

Their American names suited them perfectly. The boys never stood still. Especially Harry. He was always in a hurry to explore new ideas, rushing off to new adventures with Dash close behind.

The circus was the greatest adventure of all. True to his word, Rabbi Weiss had found seats for the whole family. They were three rows back from the center ring. Harry and Dash could see everything.

Leopold and baby Gladys giggled at the

clowns. They jumped with excitement when the elephants paraded around in a circle. Harry's parents clapped for the glittering circus horses and their riders. A girl in a white spangled dress did handstands and somersaults on the back of a pony as it cantered around the center ring. She was hardly older than Harry and Dash.

"How that little girl can ride! Simply wonderful!" Rabbi Weiss exclaimed in German as horses and riders took a bow.

Harry couldn't see what his parents were so thrilled about. "They're just horses, Papa. What's so special about jumping on and off a horse?"

"My own son doesn't like horses? Where have I failed?" Rabbi Weiss replied. He pretended to be deeply disappointed.

"Don't feel bad, Mayer," Mrs. Weiss said. "It can't be helped. We're Hungarians. Harry's an American boy. No American can ever love horses the way Hungarians do."

"I suppose you're right, Cecelia," Rabbi Weiss said with a sigh.

Harry knew his parents were teasing him. He didn't mind. They missed the Old Country in a way that their children could never understand.

*But that's past,* Harry thought. *Why waste time thinking about long ago when the future is so exciting?*

And nothing was more exciting than a tightrope walker! That's what Harry and Dash had been waiting to see ever since the circus posters went up all over Appleton.

Harry had pulled down one of the posters to keep. He stuck it on the wall of the room he and Dash shared.

Harry loved looking at that poster. The picture gave him goose bumps. It showed a man in white tights walking high above the crowd. All that stood between him and the ground far below was a thin rope. Would he keep his balance? Or would one slip plunge him to his death? How could a herd of horses be as exciting as that?

Now, as the ringmaster announced the next performer, Harry was about to see it actually happening before his eyes. The circus band fell silent. Every eye in the circus tent looked up. Monsieur Jean Weitzman, the tightrope walker, stepped out onto the high wire. Harry reached for Dash's hand. He squeezed it tight.

Monsieur Weitzman, carrying a long pole in his hands, walked across the wire. He stopped in the middle and turned around in midair. Then he walked back the way he had come. That was just the beginning.

Harry had never seen anything like it in his life. Monsieur Weitzman didn't just walk across the rope. He danced on it. He sat on a chair in the middle and pretended to read a newspaper. He carried a young woman across and back again on his shoulders while she juggled five red balls at once.

The act ended too soon. Monsieur Weitzman slid down a long rope to the ground and took his bow. The audience exploded with cheers and applause while the circus band played a lively march. Monsieur Weitzman walked around the arena, waving to the audience.

"Harry, let go! You're crushing my fingers!" Dash said.

Only then did Harry realize he was still gripping his brother's hand. Leopold's eyes were wide open. Gladys had fallen asleep in her mother's arms. Rabbi Weiss was still clapping.

"What do you think, Papa?" Harry said. "Wasn't that better than horses?"

Rabbi Weiss had to agree. "That certainly was fine," he admitted. "Still, I wish I could take you to see the circus in Budapest someday. Our performers in Hungary are the best in the world."

"I give up," Harry whispered to Dash in

English. "Everything's better in Hungary, according to Papa."

"And it gets better every time he tells us about it," Dash replied with a wink. "If it was so great over there, why did Mama and Papa come here?"

A sudden drumroll called the audience to attention. Everyone fell silent as the ringmaster strode into the center of the ring.

"Ladies and gentlemen . . . ," he began in a powerful voice. It could be heard in every corner of the circus tent. "Monsieur Jean Weitzman will now present a feat that, until this day, he has only performed before the crowned heads of Europe. Using only the power of his jaws, he will allow himself to be suspended from the highest point of the big top. Ladies and gentlemen, I do not have to remind you how dangerous this is. We must have total silence so that Monsieur

Weitzman can focus completely on what he must do."

Harry sat on the edge of his seat. He clenched his fists so tightly that his knuckles cracked. Gladys began to whimper.

"Hush, child. You must be quiet," Harry heard his mother say. Her voice seemed to come from a distance, even though she was only one seat away. He heard his father whispering prayers for the performer's safety.

Monsieur Weitzman stepped to the center of the arena. He saluted the audience. A drum rolled. A rope came down from the top of the circus tent. Monsieur Weitzman took the end of the rope in his teeth. He threw back his head, holding his arms out wide.

Harry gasped as Monsieur Weitzman rose into the air as if he were a bird flying up from the floor of the circus. Up, up he went, spinning round and round, holding on to the rope with only his teeth. Seeing such bravery left Harry breathless. How could a man find the courage to perform a feat like that? A sudden slip, an unexpected moment of weakness, would send him hurtling to his doom!

Time had never seemed so long. Minutes had never passed so slowly. Harry could not pull his eyes away from the top of the circus tent, where Monsieur Weitzman slowly turned round and round, first one way, then another, like a fish caught on a line.

At last, it was over. The rope lowered. The band began to play. Monsieur Weitzman stood beside the ringmaster, taking his bows. Harry didn't clap or cheer. He sat frozen in his seat, as if in a trance.

He felt someone shaking him. It was Dash. "Harry, are you all right?" his brother asked.

Harry nodded. It took several moments before he could speak. "That was the most amazing thing I ever saw!" he exclaimed. "How did he do it?"

"Who knows? You won't see me trying that," Dash replied. "Isn't the circus great?

Doesn't it make you wish we had our own circus here in Appleton? We wouldn't have to wait all year for the circus to come. We could go and see the show anytime we liked."

"Dash! What a great idea!" Harry exclaimed.

"What did I say?" Dash asked. He wasn't sure what Harry was talking about.

"A circus here in Appleton. A circus of our own!" Harry replied. "Only we won't have to buy tickets. We'll be the show."

# THE SECRET

It took a long time for Harry to fall asleep that night. When he finally closed his eyes, he had circus dreams.

Harry dreamed he was back in the big tent. He saw the clowns, the bareback riders, and the acrobats. All the performers had his face. It was a circus of Harrys! Then Monsieur Jean Weitzman stepped onto the high wire. But it wasn't Monsieur Weitzman at all. It was Harry Weiss, dancing, twirling, performing somersaults high in the air.

The audience watched and applauded. *They're clapping for me!* Harry thought. He looked down from the high wire and made a deep bow. To his surprise, he was bowing to himself. A Harry Weiss filled every seat under the big top. The Harrys stamped their feet, cheering, "Hooray for Harry! The greatest of all!"

Harry stood up. He threw his arms wide to accept their praise. "Thank you all! Thank you, my friends!"

"Harry! Cut that out! I'm trying to sleep." Harry heard Dash's voice, but he couldn't see him. What was Dash doing in Harry's circus? The tightrope began to wobble. Harry fought to keep his balance. He felt himself falling. Down, down, down . . .

Harry sat up in bed. The room was dark, except for a sliver of moonlight shining through the window. The Harry circus had vanished. It was all a dream, except for Dash, who was very real and very annoyed.

"Ow, Harry! Why'd you hit me in the face? That hurt! I hope you didn't give me a black eye," Dash said.

"I'm sorry, Dash," said Harry. "I didn't mean to hit you. I didn't even know I was hitting you. I was having a dream."

Dash pressed his fingers against his right eye. "It feels better now. I don't mind sharing the bed with you, but why do you have to beat me up every time you have a dream? Why don't you dream a nice dream for once?"

"This was a terrific dream, Dash!" Harry said. "I wish you could have been there with me. I was back at the circus. And guess what! I was the star of the show. I was dancing way, way up on the high wire, just like Monsieur

Weitzman did, and all the people were cheering. . . ."

Dash listened closely, his eyes wide open, as Harry told him about the dream. He described it with such detail that Dash could see it as clearly as if he'd dreamed it himself. By the time Harry finished, Dash was too excited to sleep.

"Gosh, Harry," he said, "can a dream like that come true? Could we be circus stars someday?"

"Why not?" said Harry. He leaned back on the pillows with his hands behind his head and stared at the ceiling. "Remember that story Papa told us in the synagogue last Saturday? The one about Jacob and how he dreamed about a ladder that went all the way up to heaven? Like Papa said, if you believe in dreams, there's no telling how far or how high they can take you."

"Take *us*, you mean. You're not going alone. I'm coming, too," said Dash as both boys drifted off to sleep.

Dreaming is easy. Making dreams come true is more difficult. The circus was in town until the end of the week. Harry and Dash made the most of it.

It was July, so there was no school. Papa was busy in his study or at the synagogue. Mama had her day filled with cooking, cleaning, and taking care of Gladys and Leopold. After Harry and Dash finished their chores, they could do what they liked. What they liked doing was hanging around the circus.

Harry and Dash raced to the field outside town where the circus pitched its tents. They talked with the clowns, the jugglers, the acrobats. They hauled water for the animals. They cleaned stalls. They carried bales of hay and straw. Most important for Harry, they had the chance to speak with Monsieur Weitzman, the tightrope walker.

Dressed in ordinary clothes, he seemed much smaller to Harry and Dash. "It's always

that way," Monsieur Weitzman explained. He brewed a pot of tea on the cookstove outside the mess tent. "That's why circus people love to perform. We become larger than life when the spotlight hits us."

Larger than life! Harry liked the sound of that. He wanted to be larger than life, too. "What's your secret?" he asked Monsieur Weitzman.

"Secret, Harry?" Monsieur Weitzman said. "Do you believe I have magic glue on my feet that lets me stick to the rope?"

"Well, maybe not glue, but there must be a secret," Harry said. "How else could you walk across the whole big top on a rope and not fall down?"

"Yeah," said Dash. "Tell us, Monsieur Weitzman. We won't let anyone else know. We promise."

Monsieur Weitzman smiled as he poured tea from the round yellow pot into three cups on a table. "If you really want to know, I'll tell you. Lean closer, boys. I'll whisper it in your ears."

Harry and Dash leaned over the table to

hear what Monsieur Weitzman had to say.

"Are you ready?" he began. "It's hard work and practice. Most important, you have to set your mind. If you believe you can do something and you practice every chance you get, one day you will do it. That's the secret."

"That's all there is to it? Just practice? You mean . . . if we practice hard, we can learn to walk the tightrope just like you?" Harry asked.

"That's what I said," Monsieur Weitzman replied. He tapped his forehead. "It's all up here. Oh, there are a few other things to keep in mind. Never look down. That's important. Also, start practicing on a rope that isn't too high off the ground. You're going to fall many times. Falling two feet is better than falling fifty feet." He winked at the boys as he said that.

Harry and Dash didn't wink back. What Monsieur Weitzman had just told them was too important to be a joke. It was as important as the words their father spoke in the synagogue every Saturday.

"Believe in yourself. If you think you can do it, you can." Harry repeated the words over and over in his mind as he sipped the tea. He would write them down when he got home so he wouldn't forget them. Believe in yourself, and you can make any dream come true. Believe in yourself, and you can do anything.

# PERFECT GENTLEMEN

Harry and Dash walked home from the circus. Now that Monsieur Weitzman had given them the key, they were ready to unlock the door. They were determined to become tightrope walkers.

"First, we need a place to practice," Harry decided.

"How about in the backyard?" Dash suggested. "The ground is soft from all the rain we had last month. We wouldn't get hurt if we fell. We could run a rope between the two trees where Mama strings her clothesline. What do you think, Harry?"

Harry shook his head. "It won't work."

"Huh?" Dash said. "Why? What's wrong with it?"

"Plenty," Harry said. "To start with, it's too close to the house. Mama would have a fit if she saw what we were doing. Papa would make us take down the rope and promise never, ever to do it again. And we'd have to keep that promise because Papa's a rabbi. Lying to him would be like lying to God. See what I mean?"

"Yeah," Dash agreed. "Then how are we going to find a place to practice? Do you have any ideas?"

"No," said Harry, "but there must be a place in town where we can practice without Mama and Papa finding out. Once we get really good at walking the tightrope, we'll show them what we can do. They'll realize they don't have to worry about us breaking our necks. After that, we can put on our circus!"

Dash shoved his hands in his pockets. He and Harry walked along, heads lowered. Where could they find a place to practice without anyone seeing them? They were thinking so hard that they didn't notice their teacher, Miss Purdy, coming toward them.

"Good afternoon, Harry. Good afternoon, Dash." Miss Purdy smiled as she greeted them.

The boys mumbled, "Hello," and kept walking.

"Stop right there, both of you!"

Harry and Dash stopped in their tracks. They turned around. Miss Purdy was no longer smiling. "Boys, that was extremely rude," she said. "I'm disappointed with you. Especially with you, Harry. You should know better. You should be setting an example for your younger brother."

"Gosh, Miss Purdy!" Harry exclaimed. "What did I do?"

"It's what you didn't do," Miss Purdy went on. "Remember last month in school when we talked about having good manners? Good manners aren't just for when we're in school. We have to practice them wherever we are. Now, when two young gentlemen like yourselves meet a lady, you don't mumble and go on your way, as you both did. You stop, look her in the eye, and give a pleasant greeting. You might say, 'Good day,' or, 'How nice to see you.' Either one will do."

"We know that, Miss Purdy," said Harry.

"Knowing about good manners isn't

enough, Harry," Miss Purdy said. "You have to practice them. What matters isn't what you know. It's what you do. I hope you'll both do better the next time we meet."

"We will, Miss Purdy," Harry promised. Miss Purdy smiled at the boys. She continued on her way.

"Good day. Good morning. How nice to meet you." Dash mimicked his teacher as soon as she was far enough away not to hear him. "What a fuss over nothing!"

"Maybe," said Harry. "But I just had an idea. Miss Purdy lives with her aunt, Mrs. Herrick, doesn't she?"

"Yeah," said Dash. "So what?"

"Mrs. Herrick has that old barn in the field behind her house. That might be just what we need. Come on, and do what I do." Harry took off running down the street. Dash followed at his heels.

The boys ran around the block. They turned the corner just as Miss Purdy came down the street. This time Harry was a perfect gentleman, despite being out of breath. He stopped, took off his hat, and performed a sweeping bow. It was the same one he had seen the circus performers do for the audience. Dash, copying Harry, did the same.

"Good day, Miss Purdy. How nice to see you," Harry said.

"G-good afternoon, Miss Purdy. Likewise," Dash stammered. He kept one eye on Harry and the other on Miss Purdy.

Miss Purdy smiled. She nodded to Harry first, then to Dash. "I'm proud of you boys," she said. "You see, showing good manners isn't hard. You can both be perfect gentlemen. It only takes a little effort."

"Thank you, Miss Purdy," Harry said.

"You're welcome, Harry and Dash." As

Miss Purdy turned to go, Harry suddenly asked, "Miss Purdy, do you like the circus?"

"Of course! Doesn't everybody?" she said.

"Dash and I were thinking about starting a circus of our own," Harry told her. "Just for our friends. But we need a place to practice. We don't want anybody to see us before we get really good. Can you think of anyplace we could use?"

Miss Purdy thought for a moment. "What about the old barn behind my aunt's house? Would that do? It's mostly empty. If you promise to put everything back the way you found it when you're done, I'm sure my aunt wouldn't mind."

"We promise, Miss Purdy!" Harry and Dash said together.

"Then go ahead," said Miss Purdy. "I believe the barn door is open, but if it isn't, you'll find the key hanging from a nail at the back of the garden shed."

Harry and Dash remembered their manners. "Thanks, Miss Purdy!" They took off their hats and bowed again. Then they turned on their heels and ran off down the street as fast as they could go.

# THE BARN

The old barn had stood at the edge of town since the days of the first settlers. Its beams had been cut from massive trees well over a hundred years old. Nearby was an old white house with a wide porch and a three-gabled roof. Here Miss Purdy lived with her aunt.

The barn and the house had once been part of a large dairy farm. The cows were long gone. As Appleton grew from a village into a town, most of the pasture was sold to people who wanted to build houses.

Nobody knew what to do with the old barn. Nobody cared much about it, either. It couldn't exactly be described as a ruin. Not yet, but it was heading that way.

Large flecks of red paint peeled from its boards. Rain and snow came through the holes in the roof where the wind had blown away some of the wooden shingles. Swallows nested in the eaves. Mice built homes in musty bales of straw and hay. Where mice gather, so do cats. Every cat in Appleton, wild or tame, knew the way to the barn.

Cats had no trouble getting into the barn. It was a different story for Harry and Dash. The barn door was locked, and a heavy padlock hung from the hand-forged iron hasp.

Miss Purdy had told them that the key would be hanging from a nail on the garden shed. Harry and Dash looked all around the shed, but they couldn't find it.

"Darn!" said Dash. "What'll we do now? We'll have to wait for Miss Purdy to get back. Who knows how long that'll take? I can't see why anybody would want to lock up an old barn anyway. It's not like there's stuff in there that someone would want to steal."

"Miss Purdy's aunt might have gotten tired of kids coming into her yard to fool around in her barn," Harry suggested. "Mama and Papa would do the same if we had a barn."

Dash laughed. "If we had a barn, we'd be there and not here. What are we going to do? Maybe I should run back to town to tell Miss Purdy we can't find the key. She might have another one somewhere. It could be in her purse. Maybe she put it in there the last time she came out to the barn and forgot about it."

Harry lifted the lock in his hand. He turned it over, studying it front and back.

"I don't think so," he told Dash. "This lock is really old. It must have been here when there were still cows living inside the barn. The key's probably just as big and heavy as the lock is. I can't see Miss Purdy carrying it in her purse. Somebody might have dropped it near the barn. If we look, maybe we can find it."

Harry and Dash walked around the barn together. Harry scanned the walls, looking for a nail holding a large iron key. Dash kept his eyes on the ground. Maybe the key was hidden beneath a rock. Maybe it was inside a metal box or fruit jar. They walked slowly around the barn three times. No luck.

"If it's hidden here, it's hidden good," Dash finally said. "I'll go and find Miss Purdy. Do you remember where she was going?"

"Don't go yet," said Harry. "There's something I want to try first."

He dug in his pocket and pulled out two oddly shaped lengths of metal. The first was a long piece of wire turned up at the end like the corner of a square. The second was also long and thin, but straight. It looked like a clock spring that someone had unrolled and flattened.

"What are those?" Dash asked.

"Tools," said Harry.

"Tools for what?" asked Dash.

"You'll see," Harry said.

Harry kneeled down in front of the barn door. He slipped the flat strip of metal into the keyhole. Then he worked the bent wire in after it.

"What are you doing?" Dash asked. "Are you trying to pick the lock?"

"I'm not trying," Harry replied. "I did it."

The lock popped open.

Dash stood with his mouth open. "Harry, you picked the lock! How did you learn to do that?"

Harry turned and grinned. "Mr. Hanauer at the hardware store taught me. He sells all kinds of locks there. He also knows how to open them. That's important, because people are always losing their keys."

"Like Mama and Papa," said Dash.

Harry nodded. "That's why I asked Mr. Hanauer to teach me about locks. I got tired of running to the hardware store every time Mama locked herself out."

Harry explained how his lock-picking tools worked. "This bent wire is the pick. The flat metal strip is the tension wrench. Before you can use them, you have to understand what a key does."

"It opens a lock," said Dash.

"Yeah, but how does it do that? What happens inside the lock when you turn the key?" Harry asked.

Dash shrugged. "I don't know. I can't see inside a lock."

"Neither can I," said Harry. "But I took locks apart with Mr. Hanauer. Here's what happens. A key turns a bolt. The bolt releases a latch that lets the lock open. Inside, four or five little pins fit into the bolt. Springs hold them in place. The pins stop the bolt from turning. That's why you need a key."

"What does a key do?" Dash asked. "You still haven't explained that."

Harry went on. "Every key has grooves cut into it. The high points between the grooves push the pins against the springs. When the pins are out of the way, the lock can turn."

"I get it!" cried Dash. "That's why you need the right key to open a lock. The wrong key might not fit into the keyhole. Or it might not be able to get under the pins to lift them out of the way."

"Or it might not lift them high enough so the bolt can turn," Harry added. He felt glad that Dash understood.

"So when you were picking the lock with

that bent wire thing . . . ," Dash said.

Harry finished the sentence. "I was lifting the pins out of the way so the lock could turn. See how thin the pick is? I can wiggle it around inside the lock to get at the pins. The tension wrench is flat. It fits in the key-hole like a thin key. I keep trying to turn the bolt with the tension wrench. At the same time I raise the pins one by one. When I lift the last pin out of the way, the bolt turns and the lock opens."

"Sure," said Dash. "It's easy when you know how."

"That's right," said Harry. "Knowing how is the key."

"I just have one question," Dash said. "Do you remember what happened last October? In the middle of the night, someone mysteriously opened all the locks on all the doors of all the stores on College Street. You wouldn't know anything about that, would you, Harry?"

"Me?" Harry exclaimed. He pressed his hands to his chest and opened his eyes wide. "Do I look like a burglar?"

"No," said Dash, "but you don't look like a tightrope walker, either. And you never will, unless we get busy."

"Right!" said Harry as he and Dash pulled the heavy barn doors open. "Ladies and gentlemen, step right this way. The Weiss Brothers' Circus, the greatest show under the big top, is about to begin!"

# WALKING THE TIGHTROPE

Harry and Dash peered into the empty barn. The warm air inside, heated by the summer sun, smelled of old wood and musty hay. Though the cows had been gone for decades, their odor remained. Dust motes danced in the beams of light that came down from the holes in the roof. Something skittered across their feet. Dash jumped.

"It's only a mouse," Harry said. He didn't want to admit that he'd nearly jumped, too.

The boys looked around. Where would be the best place for a tightrope? Two long aisles ran from the front of the barn to the back, with stalls on either side. Some of the stalls were still heaped with hay and straw, as if someone had expected the cows to return.

"We can put some of that straw on the ground in case we fall," Harry told Dash.

Dash wrinkled his nose. "Maybe, if we can't find anything else. Let's look in the hayloft. I'd rather land on straw that hasn't been used."

Harry and Dash continued exploring. They found an open space in the middle of the barn with a ladder leading up to the hayloft. The farmers stored hay there for their cows during the winter. A rope hung down from the roof. Harry gave it a tug. He heard a rusty squeak.

"It's attached to a pulley," Harry told Dash. "That's how they got bales of hay and straw up to the loft."

Dash looked up into the dusty shadows at the roof of the barn. "You're right," he agreed. "The ladder is the only other way up there. I can't see carrying a bale of hay up a ladder."

Harry grasped the ladder's rails. He stepped onto the first rung and began to climb.

"Be careful," Dash warned. "This ladder must be a hundred years old."

"Don't worry. It's solid," Harry said. "Those old pioneers built things to last. Like this barn. Come on up. Let's see what's in the loft."

That's where Harry and Dash found just what they needed. A length of rope hung from a nail on the wall. Harry took it down

and uncoiled it. He pulled on the rope with both hands. "This rope's as old as the ladder, but it's still strong. I think it can hold us."

"I hope so," said Dash. "Let's not put it up too high, in case it breaks." He glanced over the edge of the hayloft to the barn floor. "That's a long way to fall."

"Who's going to fall?" said Harry. "Not you. Not me. It's a challenge. We can do this."

Harry looped the coil of rope around his shoulder. He and Dash climbed back down the ladder. "Where shall we put our tight-rope?" he asked Dash.

"How about right here?" Dash said. He pointed to the two sturdy timbers at the end of the aisle between the stalls. "We can string it between these big posts. It looks like they hold up the whole barn. They should be able to hold us."

Harry and Dash set to work. Each boy took one end of the rope. They pulled it tight around the posts. They tied each end with several knots. Their tightrope crossed the barn floor at shoulder height. It was high enough to be a challenge, but not high enough for them to be seriously hurt if they fell.

"I've fallen off fences that were taller than that," said Harry. He sounded disappointed. "Can't we raise it higher?"

"Sure," said Dash. "After we get the hang of tightrope walking. Remember what Papa says. You have to learn to crawl before you can walk."

Harry laughed. "Who needs to walk? I'm ready to run!"

But Dash was right. Harry had to agree. It wouldn't hurt to take a few practice walks before raising the rope. Dash climbed back up to the loft. He opened a few of the bales of old hay that were up there. He kicked the hay down from the loft. Then he climbed back down the ladder and spread the hay on the barn floor underneath the rope.

"That's to soften our landing," Dash told Harry.

"*Your* landing," Harry replied. "I'm not going to fall."

"We'll see," said Dash. "Who's going first?"

"Me, of course! I'm the older brother," Harry answered.

Dash crouched down with his hands braced on his knees. Harry climbed up on Dash's back to reach the rope. He placed his left foot on the rope. Holding on to the post, he slowly stood up until he could put his right foot on the rope, too.

Harry stood on the tightrope. He kept

his hands on the post to steady himself.

"Let go of the post," said Dash.

"I will in just a minute," said Harry. "I'm still a little wobbly. Ready? Here I go!"

Harry let go of the post. He held out his arms, waiting for Dash to clap. Suddenly, the rope went one way and Harry went the other. The next thing he knew, he was lying on his back in the hay under the rope.

Dash ran to see if his brother was all right. "You should have seen yourself. You went flying through the air backward," Dash said. "What happened?"

"I don't know," said Harry. "One minute I was standing on the rope. The next, I was here!"

"Try it again," said Dash.

Harry and Dash kept trying to walk the tightrope. They took turns. First Harry went flying, then Dash. Again and again they climbed up. But as soon as they let go of the post, down they fell.

"We must be doing something wrong," Dash suggested. He and Harry had fallen off the rope about ten times each.

"How did Monsieur Weitzman do it?" Harry asked. He closed his eyes and tried to imagine himself back at the circus, watching the show. He suddenly heard Dash say, "I've got it!"

"What?" Harry asked.

"I figured out our mistake," Dash said. He pointed to his feet. "Look! We're wearing shoes. Monsieur Weitzman wasn't wearing shoes. He had on a pair of slippers. They matched his tights, so you hardly noticed them. He certainly wasn't wearing high-button street shoes."

"You're right!" Harry exclaimed. He felt slightly annoyed that his younger brother had remembered that detail before he did.

Harry and Dash removed their shoes and their socks. Dash went first. After all, it was his idea. He climbed up on Harry's back, steadied himself against the post, and grasped the rope between his big toe and his other toes. Then he slowly eased himself out onto the rope, an inch at a time. At last, he was holding on to the post with only his finger-tips.

Harry jumped up and down with excitement. "You're doing it, Dash! We discovered the secret! Nothing can stop us now! We'll be the greatest tightrope walkers in history!"

"I'm letting go!" Dash announced. He let go of the post. He stood on the rope for a moment, balancing all by himself. Harry cheered. The rope lurched. Dash struggled to find his balance. Over he went to land facedown in the hay.

Harry helped Dash sit up. "What a tumble! Are you all right?" he asked.

Dash spit out a mouthful of hay. "I'm glad we used hay from the loft and not from the stalls," he said. "I didn't think I'd have to eat it."

"Well, that didn't work," said Harry.

"It almost did," Dash replied. "I'm not ready to give up. We're making progress. I felt better on the rope with my bare feet than I ever did with shoes. Staying up there is hard because the rope moves every time you do. The more you try to keep your balance, the more unbalanced you become. Then off you go, flying."

"We're still missing something important," Harry decided. "What was Monsieur Weitzman doing that we're not? Think, Dash! Close your eyes. Pretend we're back at the circus. We're looking up at the tightrope. We're watching Monsieur Weitzman and he's—"

"I got it!" Dash suddenly yelled. "He wasn't trying to balance with his hands. He was holding something."

"That's it!" Harry exclaimed. "He was

carrying a long pole. He held it low, down by his waist, as he walked across the rope."

"What's special about a pole? Why should it make a difference?" Dash asked.

"I don't know," said Harry. "What do we have to lose? We can only fall off again. Let's try walking the rope with a pole and see what happens."

Harry and Dash searched all over the barn. At last, they found what they needed. Several long poles stood in a barrel near the door. Some were notched at one end for holding up a clothesline so the clothes wouldn't drag on the ground. The longest pole was different. It was five feet long and heavy.

"That looks like a curtain rod," said Dash.

"It must be," said Harry. "It's about as long as the one Monsieur Weitzman was carrying. Maybe it will work for us. Want to go first?"

Dash shook his head. "No, it's your turn, Harry. You should be the first to try it out."

Harry climbed up on Dash's back to the rope. Gripping the rope between his toes the way Dash had done, he steadied himself against the post.

"Ready," he told Dash.

Dash handed the curtain rod up to Harry. Harry grasped it in his left hand. He found his balance. Then, slowly, he let go of the post and took the pole in his right hand.

"You're doing it!" Dash cried. Harry was standing on the tightrope all by himself!

"It's the pole," Harry exclaimed. "I don't know why, but it helps me feel more steady. I'm going to try walking across."

"Do you think you can do it?" Dash asked.

"I know I can," said Harry.

Slowly, putting one foot carefully before the other, Harry began walking across the tightrope. He felt his heart pounding inside his chest. He hardly dared breathe. But he was doing it. Harry Weiss was walking across a tightrope!

The rope was only a few feet off the ground, but that didn't matter. What counted was that he'd unlocked the secret. Once he knew that, Harry realized, it didn't matter if the rope was three or three hundred feet high. He could walk any rope, any height, anywhere. All he needed was the courage to do it and the confidence to try.

Harry crossed to the other end. He turned around and began walking back. He had discovered another important secret. This one was even more important than holding a long pole. He *believed* that he could do it.

*Monsieur Weitzman was right*, Harry thought. *If you believe you can do something, it's only a matter of time before you figure out how.*

Harry walked back across the rope. He stood perfectly still, then leaped off the rope to the ground while holding the pole in his hands. Every muscle in his body ached. His legs felt like jelly. His clothes were drenched with sweat. But he had done it! He had walked the tightrope from one end to the other and back again.

"My turn next," said Dash. He took the pole from Harry.

Harry bent low to let Dash climb onto his back. "I know you can do it," he said. "It's easy. And after you're done, I want you to help me try something else."

"What?" Dash asked, steadying himself on the rope as Harry handed him the pole.

"You'll see," Harry said. "It's a secret."

# THE CHALLENGE

"**I** did it!" Dash exclaimed. Harry clapped him on the back.

"I knew you could!" Harry said. "All we had to do was figure out the secret. The rest was easy."

"I don't know that I'd call it easy," Dash replied. His words came in short gasps. He struggled to catch his breath. "We did it. That's . . . what counts. If we can . . . walk a tightrope . . . we can do anything!"

"Anything!" Harry said. "That's why I need your help. There's something else that I want to try."

"What is it?" Dash asked. He breathed more easily now.

"Remember that part of the show when Monsieur Weitzman hung from the rope by his teeth? I want to try that. I think I can do it."

"Harry, have you gone cuckoo?" Dash cried. "No. I'm not going to help you break your neck. What if something goes wrong? How could I explain it to Mama and Papa? Especially if I helped you!"

"What could go wrong, Dash?" Harry insisted. "Think about it. Can holding on to a rope with your teeth be any harder than walking a tightrope? You bite into a rope and hold on while somebody else hoists you into the air. You swing for a few minutes.

Then they lower you down. I'm telling you, Dash, we can do this."

"Leave me out of this stunt," Dash said. "Hanging by your teeth is just plain dumb. That's asking for trouble."

"If you don't want to do it, you don't have to," Harry replied. "You can be my assistant. I'll hang. You pull. All you have to do is haul on the rope."

"I'm not pulling you higher than this." Dash held his arm above his head. He drew an imaginary line in the air with his hand.

"Fine," said Harry. "All that matters is getting my feet off the ground. I'm going to see how long I can hang from the rope before I have to let go."

Harry jumped up. He took hold of the end of the rope hanging down from the pulley in front of the hayloft. "Climb up there and hold the other end," he told Dash. "Start pulling me up when you hear me yell, 'Pull!'"

Grumbling all the while, Dash climbed the ladder to the hayloft. The dust floating in the air under the barn roof made him sneeze.

"Gesundheit!" said Harry. He shaded his eyes as he looked up into the shadows.

"Thanks," said Dash. The end of the rope was tied around a peg in the wall of the barn. Dash loosened it. He took the rope in both hands and gave it a tug.

"I don't know. This rope looks really old, Harry," he called down to his brother. "It probably came to Appleton in a covered wagon. Do you really want to take the chance?"

"Sure," Harry said with a grin. "You hold on to the rope to make sure it doesn't come through the pulley. I'll tie a knot in this end."

Dash held the rope while Harry wrapped the other end over his hand. He pulled it through and around to make a loop.

"What kind of knot is that?" Dash asked.

"It's called a bowline," Harry explained. "Sailors use it. It's a slipknot that stays in place. Mr. Hanauer showed me how to tie it. He knows a lot about knots. Knots are just as interesting as locks, Dash. Do you know how many different kinds of knots there are? Hundreds! Maybe thousands. I'm going to learn to tie them all."

"Just make sure you tied this one right," Dash replied. He wrapped the rope around his arm, grasping it with both hands. "Are you ready?"

"Start pulling," Harry answered. "When I get high enough, I'm going to try to hang by my teeth. You just hold on to the rope until I give you the signal to let me down."

"Okay," said Dash. "I sure hope you know what you're doing."

"Don't I always?" said Harry. "Let's go."

Dash began pulling on the rope. Harry held tight to the loop in the bowline as if he were chinning himself up. Higher and higher he rose, until he was four feet off the ground. His toes were level with the tops of the stalls.

"Hold me right here!" Harry called to Dash. While Dash held the rope in place, Harry raised himself with both arms until his mouth was level with the loop. He leaned forward and took the rope between his teeth.

Ugh! Harry hadn't thought about what it might mean to take that old rope into his mouth. The bristles felt like sandpaper. They scratched his tongue and lips. He tasted dust, moldy hay, and mice. Disgusting!

But Harry held on. He was determined to prove he could do whatever Monsieur Weitz-man could do. A bad-tasting rope wouldn't stop him.

Harry sank his teeth into the bristles. His mouth filled with spit. It dribbled down his chin until his neck and the whole front of his shirt were wet. This was the moment. Harry was ready. He braced himself, took a deep breath. He let go with his hands.

Harry swung in midair, suspended only by the grip of his teeth. His body turned first to the right, then to the left. He felt as if he were trying to hold on to a moving train. His body bent backward to balance the pull, as if he were a bow that an invisible archer was using to shoot an arrow. His teeth ached. His eyes teared. Buckets of spit ran down his chin, but his mouth felt dry and dusty.

This was horrible, much worse than he

had ever imagined. And yet, he'd been hanging for less than a minute. How had Monsieur Weitzman hung for so long? How had he made it seem so easy?

Harry couldn't answer those questions. But he did know the answer to the most important one. How long was he going to hang here?

*Until I count to a hundred,* Harry told himself. He began counting. He couldn't speak, but he could say the words in his mind. *One . . . two . . . three . . . four . . .* At the same time, he focused on one single idea. Hold on!

"Harry! That's enough. How long are you going to do this?" Dash called.

Harry ignored him. *Thirty-six . . . thirty-seven . . .*

Dash became worried. "Come on, Harry. I'm going to let you down."

Harry looked up into Dash's face. Harry couldn't speak the words. He couldn't talk. Instead, he brought all his determination into one thought. It passed between Harry's eyes and those of his brother. *Don't give up, Dash! Don't quit on me! If I can hold on, so can you. Don't let me down!*

Dash understood. "You're crazy. I don't like this one bit. But I won't let you down until you tell me to," he promised.

Harry forced as much of a smile as he dared. Then he waved his arms to signal to Dash. *Pull me higher!*

"No! Harry, why? What are you trying to prove?" Dash protested.

Harry waved his arms again. *Higher!*

Dash began hauling on the rope. Whether it made sense or not, Harry was calling on him to do his part. They were more than brothers. Harry and Dash were a team. They

had always counted on each other. This time would be no different.

The rusty pulley squealed. Harry rose above the stalls. He was almost to the roof of the barn. His head was only a few feet below the rafters.

Harry closed his eyes. He felt like a sponge that had been wrung dry. His spit stopped flowing. The bristly rope tasted worse than ever. He felt as if his teeth were being yanked out of his jaws. But, despite all that, he had kept the count. He was almost there. *Ninety-three . . . ninety-four . . .*

A few seconds left! If he could only hold on a little longer. Harry dug his teeth into the rope. He threw back his head. *Yes . . . yes . . . yes!* he told himself. *Only a little more. I'm almost home. I can do this.* He kept repeating those words in his mind over and over again.

*I can . . . I can . . . I can . . .*

Harry tasted something wet and salty gushing in his mouth. It wasn't spit. He couldn't taste the rope anymore. He felt as if his jaws were being forced open with a crowbar. He bit down, trying to hold on to the rope. But it wasn't there.

There was only the gushing salty taste overflowing his mouth. He heard someone scream. Was it Dash? And then he was flying backward, like another barn swallow, down away from the shadowy rafters at the roof of the barn.

Down . . . down . . . down.

# Two Front Teeth

If Harry could have seen himself, he would have screamed, too. He lay on his back on the thick pile of hay and straw where he fell. Floods of that salty liquid filled his mouth.

Harry thought it was bad-tasting spit from the rope. He tried to swallow it, but there was more and more. Harry raised his hand to his lips. He stared at his fingers. They were covered with blood—his own blood. It poured from his mouth.

"Harry! You're alive," Dash was shouting as he climbed down the ladder. "I thought you were dead. Stay right there. Don't move. I'll run and get help." Dash turned and ran out the barn door.

"Don't scare everybody. I'll be okay," Harry tried to call after him. He discovered that his mouth didn't work right. It wasn't just that he kept spitting blood. His words sounded strange. They hissed and whistled so badly that he could hardly understand himself.

Suddenly, he realized what was wrong. Harry brought his tongue to his lips and felt for his two front teeth. There was only an empty space. His two front teeth were gone!

"My teeth!" Harry groaned. The words came out "My feef!"

He felt sick to his stomach, and not from swallowing dust and rope and blood. He wasn't okay. He would never be okay again. Now he realized why he had fallen from the rope. His strength hadn't given out. His teeth had. His weight on the rope had torn them out of his mouth.

Harry tried to stand up, but he became dizzy and had to sit back down. He tried again. This time he struggled to his hands and knees. His teeth lay somewhere in the heap of hay and straw scattered over the barn floor.

Harry had to find them. The doctor might know how to stick them back in. Or Mama could sew them in, just as she fixed the holes in his socks and trousers. Maybe Papa knew special prayers that would help a boy grow new teeth.

Harry tried saying prayers himself as he scrabbled in the straw. He had never thought about his teeth at all until he lost them. Now they had become the two most important things in his life.

"Somebody help me," Harry groaned. What came out sounded more like "Fombody hep me."

Help was on its way. Dash had run all the way home, screaming at the top of his voice. "Help! Harry's hurt!" Dash's cries alerted the whole town.

Heads popped out of stores and houses to see what was wrong. A man came out of the barbershop with his face half shaved. The barber chased after him, still holding his razor. Sheriff Lennon came running from the jail. Mr. Hanauer dashed into the hardware store. He grabbed a crowbar in case Harry had gotten stuck and something needed to be pried loose to free him.

Trainmen from the rail yard, clerks from the telegraph office, and students from the college all came to help. The performers and workers from the circus came running, too. Dr. Reeve grabbed his black doctor's bag and climbed into his buggy. He passed Miss Purdy as he drove down the street.

"Get in," he said. "Some boy's in trouble
down by the old barn at your place."

"Oh, dear!" Miss Purdy cried. "I hope it
isn't Harry!"

Sheriff Lennon and a man passing by on the street had already carried Harry out of the barn by the time Dr. Reeve and Miss Purdy arrived. They set him down on the grass. Harry was still in a daze, and he could hardly speak. The sunlight hurt his eyes. He blinked. Dash kneeled down next to him to shade Harry's eyes with his cap.

Dr. Reeve pushed through the crowd, carrying his doctor's bag. Rabbi and Mrs. Weiss followed him. Mama Weiss cried out when she saw Harry lying on the ground with blood all over his face.

"My son! My poor Harry is dead!" she shrieked in German.

Rabbi Weiss comforted her. "No, Mama. Harry is still alive. We won't know how badly he's hurt until Dr. Reeve examines him. Pray that he will be all right."

Mrs. Weiss's lips moved quietly. She

whispered a prayer for Harry. Everyone in the crowd waited to hear what Dr. Reeve would say.

Harry looked up at the doctor. "Will I be all right?" he tried to say. His mouth was so swollen that he could hardly get the words out.

"Lie still. Don't try to talk," the doctor said. He moved Harry's arms and legs, looking for broken bones. He checked his eyes and examined his head. "How many fingers am I holding up?" he asked Harry.

"Three," Harry tried to say.

The doctor nodded. "That's right. What's your name?"

"Harry Weiss."

"Where do you live?"

"Appleton, Wisconsin."

"What day is today?"

"Thursday. July seventh."

"Very good," said Dr. Reeve. He turned to Harry's parents. "He's had a knock on the head, but there are no bones broken. I can't find any serious damage. He'll be all right." The doctor turned back to Harry. "Now open your mouth so I can see what's going on in there."

Harry opened his mouth wide. The doctor frowned. "You knocked out your two front teeth! How did you do that to yourself?"

Harry couldn't answer. He felt too dizzy to speak. Dash answered for him.

"We were teaching ourselves how to walk a tightrope. We did it, too. Then after that, Harry wanted to learn another trick. He wanted to hang from a rope with his teeth."

"That solves the mystery," Dr. Reeve said. "Where did you boys get a crazy idea like that?"

"It's not crazy!" said Dash. "We saw Monsieur Weitzman do it in the circus. Harry wanted to learn how to do it, too."

Some of the people in the crowd began laughing. Even Dr. Reeve found it hard not to smile. Mama Weiss burst into tears. Rabbi Weiss became angry.

He scolded the boys in German. "And you, Dash, went along with such a foolish idea! Must you boys do everything you see? What will you try next? Swallowing swords?

Eating fire? Climbing into a cage with lions and tigers? I'm sorry I took you to the circus. Unless you two start showing some sense, we'll never go again."

"That would be a pity," someone answered in German. Rabbi Weiss turned around to see who it was. Harry looked up, too. He saw Monsieur Weitzman. He wore an ordinary coat and tie and carried a bucket. "I'm terribly sorry this happened," he said in English. "I brought some cold water from the well. It may help."

"Thank you. That's just what Harry needs," said Dr. Reeve. The doctor dipped his handkerchief in the bucket. He wiped the blood from Harry's mouth.

"Take some water and spit it out," he told Harry, handing him a tin cup. Harry sipped from the cup and spit. The water came out pink. It was the same color as the embroidered flowers on Mama's best tablecloth, Harry noticed. "Now open wide." Harry opened his mouth so Dr. Reeve could examine his teeth.

"How old is Harry?" the doctor asked Rabbi Weiss.

"Seven. He'll be eight in March," Harry's father answered.

"Then he'll be all right," the doctor said. "He's lost two teeth, but they were only baby teeth. His permanent teeth will grow in soon. Nobody will ever know he had two teeth missing, unless he decides to go swinging from ropes again."

"Don't worry. That won't happen," Monsieur Weitzman said. He kneeled down to have a talk with Harry and Dash. Harry couldn't speak. He had to keep the cold, wet handkerchief pressed against the empty space in his gums to stop the bleeding. But

Dash could speak for him. Dash always knew what Harry was thinking.

"Listen, boys," Monsieur Weitzman began. "A trick may look easy. That doesn't mean it *is* easy. There's also something else to remember. What you think you see may not be what's really happening."

"What does that mean?" Dash asked. Harry nodded. He had the same question.

Monsieur Weitzman looked around to see if anyone else was listening. The crowd at the barn had broken up. Most of the people began walking back to town once they learned that Harry would be all right. Harry's parents were talking with Dr. Reeve and Miss Purdy. Satisfied, Monsieur Weitzman took what looked like a shoe heel out of his pocket and showed it to the boys.

"What's that?" Dash asked.

"It's the secret to the rope trick," Monsieur

Weitzman whispered. "It's a special rubber plate that's made to fit my teeth. I attach it to the rope, then bite on it."

"So you're biting on the plate, not the rope," Dash said.

Harry's eyes opened wide. Now he understood. Biting down on a rubber plate with all your teeth had to be easier than trying to bite on a rope with your two front ones. His two front teeth could never have held his whole weight for long. Why hadn't he realized that before? It made so much sense.

"Why didn't you tell us about the plate?" Dash asked Monsieur Weitzman.

"You didn't say you were going to try hanging from a rope by your teeth," Monsieur Weitzman replied. "You just told me that you wanted to practice tightrope walking. Had you told me you wanted to try the rope trick, I would have told you not to."

Then Harry spoke. He pulled the handkerchief out of his mouth and said the words slowly so Monsieur Weitzman could understand him. "Then none of it's true," he said with great disappointment. "You cheated! It's just a trick. Anyone can do it."

"No, that's not how it is at all!" Monsieur Weitzman told Harry and Dash. "Can anyone do it? I don't think so. How many people do you know who would hang thirty feet in the air, holding on to a rope with just their teeth? It takes skill, courage, and practice. I did what I promised. I hung in the air by my teeth." He winked at Harry and Dash. "I just didn't do it the way you expected."

"I'm starting to understand what you mean," Harry murmured. "What matters is what you do, not how you do it."

"That's part of it," Monsieur Weitzman exclaimed. "There's also something else. You don't just rush off to perform a feat. You study it. You learn about it. You talk to people who have done it. If you can, you practice with them. You plan ahead so that you're ready to deal with anything that might go wrong. Yes, imagination and courage are important. But so is preparation. Being prepared will save your life when the unexpected happens. And it will happen. You can count on that."

"I already found that out," Harry said through his missing teeth.

"Accidents happen," Monsieur Weitzman replied. "If you learn the lesson the hard way, you'll never forget it. Once you've mastered that lesson, you can leap through fiery hoops and you can tame lions. You can do whatever you set your mind to doing. The rest will come in good time, Harry. One day, I have no doubt, you'll be a showman."

# UNFINISHED BUSINESS

Not everyone agreed. Harry's parents didn't. Seeing Harry lying on the grass, his face smeared with blood, they feared he had been badly hurt. Once Dr. Reeve told them Harry would be fine, anger replaced fear.

"How could you be so foolish!" Rabbi Weiss shouted. "You're the older brother, Harry! Mother and I count on you to set an example for Dash. What kind of example is this? Swinging from ropes like a monkey!"

"Don't be so hard on him, Mayer. He and Dash were only having fun," Harry's mother pleaded. "They were trying to perform the tricks they saw in the circus. They imagined themselves to be circus stars. Don't you remember when you were young and all the things you imagined yourself doing?"

"I never imagined myself hanging from a rope like an ape!" Rabbi Weiss shot back.

Harry's mother smiled. "Perhaps not. But didn't you have some other dreams? Like riding horses bareback in the arena? Shall I tell the boys about them?"

Harry and Dash leaned forward to listen. As far as they knew, their father had always been a rabbi. He had wanted to be a rabbi since he was as old as they were. At least, that's what they believed. Maybe it wasn't so. Did grown-ups have secrets? Had their father once dreamed of being a circus rider?

"Never mind!" Harry's father said. His voice was stern, but the twinkle in his eye let the boys know their punishment wouldn't be so bad. Mother had won the argument, as she always did. Their father had not forgotten what it was like to be young. Or to have dreams.

"It's bad enough that you frightened Mother and me out of our wits. You scared the whole town, too."

"And what of Miss Purdy's barn?" said Harry's mother. "You left a mess. There's blood, straw, and hay all over the place. Who is going to clean it up?"

Harry and Dash hung their heads. "We will, Mama. We're sorry, Papa. It won't happen again," said Harry.

"Then that will be your punishment," said Rabbi Weiss. "If you clean up the barn and put everything back the way it was, we'll speak no more of this. And there will be no more fooling around with ropes, either walking on them or hanging from them."

"Yes, Papa," Harry and Dash agreed.

The next morning dawned bright and sunny, a perfect summer day for having fun. The children of Appleton, Wisconsin, were already making plans for going fishing, playing ball, riding horses, rolling hoops through the street, and dozens of other ways to enjoy themselves. All the children . . . except two. Harry and Dash. The morning sun found them trudging along the street to Miss Purdy's house.

Harry carried a rake over his shoulder. His mouth hurt, and it was hard to speak clearly without his two front teeth. His body was bruised from the fall. However, as much as Harry moaned and groaned, Rabbi Weiss

ignored him. Harry's injuries weren't so serious that they should prevent him from
cleaning up the barn.

Dash walked beside Harry, carrying a
broom. He didn't think it was fair that he
should have to clean up the barn, too, when
Harry had been the one who tried to hang
from the rope. This argument did not im-
press Harry and Dash's parents one bit.

"Doing a few chores won't kill you,"
Mama Weiss said. "It's time you boys learned
to clean up after yourselves."

If Mama with her kind heart was not
going to save them, no one would. Harry
and Dash walked slowly. All the children in
Appleton knew where they were going. Each
one, it seemed, had something to say.

"Hey, Harry! Show us how to whistle!"
the boys yelled.

"Let's see your teeth!" the girls called.

They laughed and hooted, but it was all in fun. Harry had to bear it.

Harry and Dash knocked on Miss Purdy's front door. Miss Purdy smiled to see them. "Hello, boys! What brings you here this fine morning? You're not going to hang from any more ropes, are you, Harry? I hope not. I feel terrible about your poor teeth."

"It's not so bad, Miss Purdy. They'll grow back," Harry said, speaking slowly so Miss Purdy could understand him. As hard as he tried, he couldn't help lisping and whistling.

"You don't have to worry about us hanging from ropes. Or walking on them, either," Dash added. "Mama and Papa told us to keep our feet on the ground or we'll never get to go to the circus again. They told us we had to clean up the mess in the barn and put everything back the way it was. That's why we're here."

"I don't think you left such a terrible mess," Miss Purdy told them. "Harry was hurt. We all were frightened. We all had more important things to attend to than a pile of hay in an old barn. I'll tell you what—

why don't you get started? I was about to bake some oatmeal cookies. They should be done by the time you finish."

"Thank you, Miss Purdy!" Harry and Dash exclaimed at once. "We'll get the barn cleaned up right away." They hurried off to the barn, carrying the rake and broom.

"It may be locked," Miss Purdy called after them. "Come back if you need the key."

The barn door was locked, but Harry didn't need the key. It took him less than a minute to pick the lock. He and Dash began raking up straw and hay.

"It sure is a big pile," Dash said. "I wish we had a wheelbarrow. We could carry it out faster if we had a wheelbarrow."

"Maybe there's one in the barn," Harry said. "I'll look." He had hardly turned down the aisle when he heard Dash cry out.

"Harry! Come here! Look what I found!"

Harry came running. He saw Dash holding up a pair of rings connected by a few links of chain. Handcuffs!

"Where'd you find those?" Harry asked.

"They were in the hay pile. They weren't there when we were playing with the rope yesterday. Where did they come from?"

Harry took the handcuffs from Dash. He turned them over in his hands. "I think I know," he finally said. "Sheriff Lennon must have dropped them when he bent down to carry me outside."

"We'll have to bring them back," said Dash.

"Yeah," Harry agreed. "But not right away. I want to study them first."

"What for?" Dash asked. "Are you planning to have Sheriff Lennon lock you up?"

"No," Harry said. "Handcuffs are interesting. They're just another kind of lock. I wonder how hard it would be to get out of them."

"Plenty hard," said Dash.

"Maybe not. Let's find out," said Harry. He placed his hands behind his back. "Put the cuffs on me, Dash. Make them as tight as you can."

Dash shook his head. "Oh no, Harry! This is just going to get us in trouble, and we're in trouble already. You're going to get locked in those handcuffs. How are you going to get out of them? We don't even have the key."

"I don't need a key," Harry said. "And I will get out of them. Try me!"

"Okay," Dash said as he snapped the handcuffs over Harry's wrists. He tightened them as far as they would go. "Now let's see you get out of them!"

"Turn around and count to three," said Harry.

Dash turned around and closed his eyes. "One ... two ..."

"Here are the cuffs," said Harry.

Dash opened his eyes. Harry stood before him, holding Sheriff Lennon's handcuffs. They were still locked, but Harry had gotten free.

"How did you do that?" Dash gasped,

amazed. "How did you get out of those hand-cuffs without opening them?"

"I remembered what Monsieur Weitzman told me yesterday. I did what I promised, but not what you expected," Harry explained. "Look at these handcuffs, Dash. They're made for a man's wrists, not a boy's. As soon as I saw them, I knew they'd be too big to fit me, even if you locked them all the way. I spread my fingers wide when you were putting them on so they wouldn't fall off."

"And I never noticed how big they were!" Dash said. "That's really smart, Harry."

"I had them off before you even started counting," Harry said.

There wasn't time to talk after that. Harry slipped the handcuffs into his pocket as Miss Purdy came through the door with a jug of cold milk and a tray heaped with oatmeal cookies. Harry, Dash, and Miss Purdy had a picnic in the barn. Then Miss Purdy got the wheelbarrow from the garden. She helped the boys carry away the last of the hay and straw.

Harry and Dash made their way home down College Street in the bright noon sunshine. Harry's pockets were full of oatmeal cookies and his head was full of plans.

"We'll get busy as soon as we get home. I have lots of ideas I want to try for our circus," he told Dash.

"Circus?" Dash exclaimed. "What are you talking about, Harry? How are we going to have a circus? Papa has forbidden us to get on a tightrope. You don't have any front teeth. Forget it. Our circus days are over."

"Not at all," Harry said. "We don't need to walk a tightrope. Every circus in the world has a tightrope artist. And I might hang from a rope one day. But I have to wait for my new teeth to grow in. So I was wondering, what else could we try?"

Dash shrugged. "I don't know. What else is there? Horses? Elephants? Sword swallowing?"

Harry shook his head. He already had a plan. Harry dug between the cookies in his pocket for what he wanted. He twirled what he found around his finger so Dash could see.

"I was thinking about handcuffs."

# Author's Note

This story is based on actual events in the life of Harry Houdini (1874–1926), perhaps the greatest magician and escape artist of all time. Harry, whose real name was Ehrich Weiss, used the stage name "Houdini" as a tribute to Jean-Eugène Robert-Houdin, a famous French magician of the nineteenth century. Harry's brother Dash (1876–1945) also became a celebrated magician. He performed under the name "Hardeen."

Harry Houdini became fascinated with locks as a boy in Appleton. One night, to challenge himself, he picked the locks on all the doors of all the stores along College Street. His skill was so well known that the sheriff asked him to open the handcuffs for a prisoner scheduled to be released. The sheriff had lost the key, and the prisoner didn't want to wait around while he looked for it.

Harry's boyhood interest in locks became a lifelong passion. As "the Handcuff King," he challenged audiences and police departments all over the world to come up with a lock or shackle he couldn't escape from. No one ever did.

# ABOUT THE AUTHOR

**E**ric A. Kimmel grew up in Brooklyn, New York. He is the award-winning author of several well-known children's books, including *Anansi and the Moss-Covered Rock* and the Caldecott Honor Book *Hershel and the Hanukkah Goblins*, as well as the Stepping Stone books *A Horn for Louis* and *A Picture for Marc*. He and his wife, Doris, live in Portland, Oregon.

**If you liked *A Spotlight for Harry*,**

**read Eric A. Kimmel's**

# A Horn for Louis

Louis saw guitars, trombones, and clarinets hanging in the window. He saw saxophones, violins, and banjos. And one trumpet!

The trumpet looked new. Its polished brass shined. Louis stood on tiptoe. He pressed his nose against the window. The trumpet was the most beautiful horn Louis had ever seen. Then he looked at the price tag.

Twenty-five dollars!

Louis's shoulders sagged. He looked at the silver dollar in his hand. That trumpet might as well have been made of gold.